Usborne
Phonics Readers
Shark in the park

Phil Roxbee Cox

Illustrated by Stephen Cartwright

Edited by Jenny Tyler

Language consultant: Marlynne Grant
BSc, CertEd, MEdPsych, PhD, AFBPs, CPsychol

There is a little yellow duck to find on every page.

First published in 2006 by Usborne Publishing Ltd., Usborne House, 83-85 Saffron Hill, London EC1N 8RT, England. www.usborne.com
Copyright © 2006, 2002 Usborne Publishing Ltd.

All rights reserved. No part of this publication may be reproduced, stored in a retrieval system or transmitted in any form or by any means, electronic, mechanical, photocopying, recording or otherwise without the prior permission of the publisher. The name Usborne and the devices ⚛ 🎈 are Trade Marks of Usborne Publishing Ltd. Printed in China. UE. First published in America in 2006.

Pup is in the park.

"There's a shark
in the park!"
Pup barks.

Pup
wakes
Fat Cat.

She meows,
"Why did
you bark?"

"There's a shark
in the park!"
Pup barks.

Big Pig is lighting a fire.
What a bright spark!

"There's a shark
in the park!"
Pup barks.

Hen is with her pad and pens.
She makes bright squiggles
and marks.

"There's a shark
in the park!"
Pup barks.

"It has sharp,
pointy...

Sam Sheep is asleep,
where it's dark.

"There's a shark
in the park!"
Pup barks.

"A shark?" meows Fat Cat.

"A shark?" grunts Big Pig.

"A shark?"
clucks Hen.

"ZZZZZZ,"
snores Sam
Sheep (still
fast asleep).

13

"Yes, a shark. There's a
SHARK in the PARK!"
Pup barks.

"Make your way to the lake!"

Up pops Jake Snake.

There's no shark in the park!

It's Jake Snake and his rubber ring!